Beantown Pals
Joyride

© Beantown Pals Holdings 2023

Illustrated By: Lizette Duvenage

Written By:
Tom Hayes & Tammy Pooler

Beantown Pals
Joyride

Written by Tom Hayes & Tammy Pooler
Illustrated by Lizette Duvenage
Editing and Book Design by Mary Noden

Published by Beantown Pals Holdings
a subsidiary of Wooden Leg Productions

ISBN 978-1-961806-01-6

Copyright 2023 Beantown Pals Holdings
All Rights Reserved

Scanning, uploading, or distribution of this book electronically or any other means, without the permission of Wooden Leg Productions, is illegal and punishable by law. To obtain permissions, contact:
Amanda Nelson, Esq.
Artium Amore, PLLC
One Mill Street, #151
Dover, NH 03820

Your support for the author's and publisher's rights is appreciated.

More
Beantown Pals

Beantown Pals is the property of Beantown Pals Holdings
a subsidiary of Wooden Leg Productions.

The Beantown Pals stories and adventures take place in the whimsical land of
Beantown. It is a food inspired community where the descendants of Jack's magic
beans live. In this community, beans of all colors and walks of life, live and work
together in carton skyscrapers, cozy teapots, and gleaming cheese graters. Even their
vehicles are items found in the kitchen! .

Joyride is the first book in the Beantown Pals series. Bucky is asked to take Laddie the
Firetruck to the Beantown Garage for maintenance. Betty invites herself along for the
drive and takes them on a wild and crazy joyride through the heart of Beantown.
Like all of our stories, Bucky and Betty get things wrong, they get things right ,
and they learn important life lessons along the way.

For more Beantown Pals audio, animation, toy and book adventures,
visit www.beantownpals.com

Use your Bean. Trust your Heart. Build your Character.

One Saturday morning, before the sun was high in the sky, Beantown Garage was busy. Quite busy. Today was the last day for beans to get their motor-spoons inspected before the town's big race.

The phone rang and Boss, the Garage's owner, answered.

"Beantown Garage, Boss speaking," he said. The clatter of hammers and whine of drills made it difficult for Boss to hear.

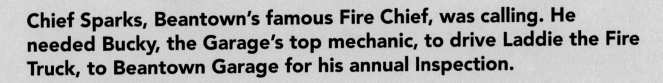

Chief Sparks, Beantown's famous Fire Chief, was calling. He needed Bucky, the Garage's top mechanic, to drive Laddie the Fire Truck, to Beantown Garage for his annual Inspection.

"Just remind Bucky that no one is allowed to ride with Laddie but him," said Chief Sparks. "We don't want any problems."

"Sure," said Boss. "I'll send him right over."

"Bucky," called Boss. "Chief needs you to bring Laddie here for his annual check-up. Robo can finish work on that motor-spoon."

Bucky grinned. The entire morning, he had dreamed of leaving the Garage early to be with his best friend, Betty.

"Sure Boss, I'll have Betty pick me up and drive me to the station."

"Okay," Boss said. "Remember, no one else is allowed to ride in Laddie. Not even Betty. Only You."

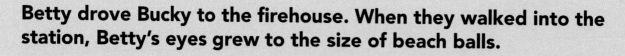

Betty drove Bucky to the firehouse. When they walked into the station, Betty's eyes grew to the size of beach balls.

"Wow!" she said. "So, this is Laddie! I've never been this close to him. He's beautiful. Can I have a ride?"

Bucky felt his stomach flip. He was afraid this would happen. "I don't think so, Betty. Chief Sparks wants no one but me to drive Laddie to the Garage. He doesn't want any trouble."

Betty brushed her hands over Laddie's smooth, red paint job.

"Wow, Bucky, he feels so smooth! I'm sure Laddie won't mind."

Bucky held his ground and repeated what Boss had said while Betty continued to admire Laddie. Next, she climbed Laddie's stairs and sat inside his cab.

Bucky stammered, "Ah, Betty, I don't think that's a good idea."

Betty reassured Bucky everything would be just fine.

Bucky couldn't resist Betty's charm. He tried to tell himself nothing could go wrong, but his stomach told him something else.

In moments, Bucky found himself riding down Main Street with Betty as Laddie's driver. Betty was excited. Bucky was not. He warned Betty not to touch anything.

Betty admired all the shiny buttons and dials and selected Laddie's siren button. She pressed it. The siren blared. Main Street shook. Beans of all shapes and sizes rattled and covered their ears.

Bucky yelled "Don't Touch Anything!"

Betty promised not to touch anything.

Bucky's stomach twitched.

Next, Betty found Laddie's blaster button. She pressed it. Again, Main Street shook. Dogs barked, lady beans screamed, old beans jumped, and kid beans pumped their arms for more. Betty gave them more.

Betty soon found Laddie's horn button. She pressed it. Again, Main Street shook.

Bucky screamed.

Betty promised.

Bucky's stomach groaned.

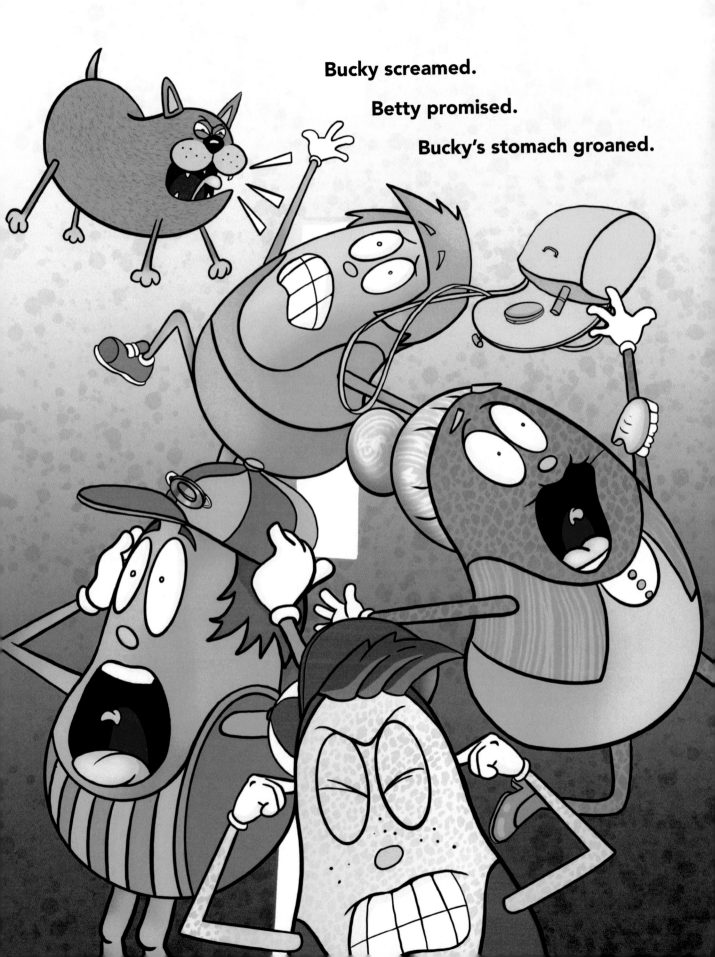

Seconds later, Betty found the button for Laddie's ladder. She pressed it. Soon, the ladder rose and climbed. It hit the beautiful, old trees lining Main Street's sidewalks.

Trunks cracked. Limbs broke. Leaves fell.

Bucky yelled.

Betty promised.

Bucky's stomach growled.

Again, Bucky heard a siren. He stared at Betty. She wasn't pressing any buttons. He looked in Laddie's mirrors and found the siren. Officer Lima's cruiser, Chase, was fast approaching.

Trouble was on the way.

Betty pulled over and covered her eyes.
Officer Lima walked their way.

Officer Lima wrote Bucky and Betty a warning and told them, as punishment, they would need to serve community time.

Officer Lima returned to his cruiser, got in, and drove away.

Bucky was upset. He should have insisted on following Chief Sparks's instructions and driven Laddie himself. Betty was upset too. She should not have insisted on riding with Bucky. Betty apologized for not listening.

Bucky started Laddie's engine
and headed for Beantown Garage.
He and Betty had made many mistakes and upset many
Beantown citizens. Now they must face the consequences.

Introducing our next **Beantown Pals** book:

A Day at The Fire Station

In Joyride, Bucky and Betty made a lot of trouble for Beantown. Now they must repay the Beantown citizens by spending a Saturday cleaning the Beantown Fire Station.

What could **possibly** go wrong?